HOTSCOTCH
MYTHS

Thor's Hammer

First published in 2008 by
Franklin Watts
338 Euston Road
London
NW1 3BH

Franklin Watts Australia
Level 17/207 Kent Street
Sydney
NSW 2000

A CIP catalogue record for this book is available
from the British Library.

ISBN 978 0 7496 7997 2 (hbk)
ISBN 978 0 7496 8005 3 (pbk)

Series Editor: Melanie Palmer
Series Advisor: Dr Barrie Wade
Series Designer: Peter Scoulding

Printed in China

Franklin Watts is a division of
Hachette Children's Books,
an Hachette Livre UK company
www.hachettelivre.co.uk

Thor's Hammer

by Maggie Moore and Tim Archbold

FRANKLIN WATTS
LONDON•SYDNEY

Thor woke up with a nasty shock.
"Who's taken my hammer?"
he said, angrily.

Everyone was scared. Thor's mighty hammer was magic. It kept them safe from evil giants.

7

"Only a wicked giant could have stolen it," said Loki. "I'll go and find out where it is."

Loki used his magical powers to change into a bird. He flew swiftly to the land of the giants.

Thrym, king of the giants, stood at the entrance to the giants' lair. "What do you want?" he boomed. "Thor's hammer," Loki replied.

"Thor can only have it back if
Freya marries me," said Thrym.

Loki flew back to find Freya.
She was the most beautiful
of all the goddesses.

12

"Thrym will keep Thor's hammer
until you marry him," said Loki.
"I won't marry an ugly, old giant,"
cried Freya.

"I want my hammer and I'll get it back," growled Thor. "Freya, you will not go to Thrym, I will!"

Thor ordered a bridal dress and
veil large enough to fit him.

When it was ready, he put on the
dress and covered his face with
the veil. Everyone laughed.

"Don't worry," said Thor.
"Giantesses are all ugly,
so I will look beautiful."

Loki and Thor travelled to Thrym's lair. "Welcome, my beautiful bride," said Thrym. "I have prepared a wedding feast for you. But first, let me see your face."

"No," said Loki, "not until the wedding. She is very shy."

They all sat down to eat the feast.
Thor ate an ox, eight salmon
and a goat.

21

He drank two barrels of beer. "She
is hungry and thirsty!" said Thrym.

"Yes," said Loki. "She has been so
nervous about the wedding that she
hasn't eaten or drunk for a week."

Thrym smiled. "Lower your veil, Freya, so that I can see your eyes," he said.

Thor lowered his veil a little.

His red, fiery eyes peered out.

"Her eyes are very red," said Thrym.
"Oh yes," said Loki. "She hasn't
slept for a week either."

26

"I think it is time to marry
now," said Thrym, smiling.
"We need the hammer first,"
said Loki. "It will bring luck!"

Thrym grumbled, but went to get the hammer. He held it up to celebrate the wedding day.

Thor grabbed the hammer. Then he ripped off his veil and gown. "This is my hammer!" he roared.

There was a great battle. Thor
hurled the hammer at Thrym and
killed him. No giant was left alive!

Thor and Loki returned home as heroes. "No one will ever take my hammer again," Thor promised.

Hopscotch has been specially designed to fit the requirements of the Literacy Framework. It offers real books by top authors and illustrators for children developing their reading skills. There are 63 Hopscotch stories to choose from:

Marvin, the Blue Pig
ISBN 978 0 7496 4619 6

Plip and Plop
ISBN 978 0 7496 4620 2

The Queen's Dragon
ISBN 978 0 7496 4618 9

Flora McQuack
ISBN 978 0 7496 4621 9

Willie the Whale
ISBN 978 0 7496 4623 3

Naughty Nancy
ISBN 978 0 7496 4622 6

Run!
ISBN 978 0 7496 4705 6

The Playground Snake
ISBN 978 0 7496 4706 3

"Sausages!"
ISBN 978 0 7496 4707 0

Bear in Town
ISBN 978 0 7496 5875 5

Pippin's Big Jump
ISBN 978 0 7496 4710 0

Whose Birthday Is It?
ISBN 978 0 7496 4709 4

The Princess and
the Frog
ISBN 978 0 7496 5129 9

Flynn Flies High
ISBN 978 0 7496 5130 5

Clever Cat
ISBN 978 0 7496 5131 2

Moo!
ISBN 978 0 7496 5332 3

Izzie's Idea
ISBN 978 0 7496 5334 7

Roly-poly Rice Ball
ISBN 978 0 7496 5333 0

I Can't Stand It!
ISBN 978 0 7496 5765 9

Cockerel's Big Egg
ISBN 978 0 7496 5767 3

How to Teach a Dragon Manners
ISBN 978 0 7496 5873 1

The Truth about those
Billy Goats
ISBN 978 0 7496 5766 6

Marlowe's Mum and
the Tree House
ISBN 978 0 7496 5874 8

The Truth about
Hansel and Gretel
ISBN 978 0 7496 4708 7

The Best Den Ever
ISBN 978 0 7496 5876 2

ADVENTURES

Aladdin and the Lamp
ISBN 978 0 7496 6692 7

Blackbeard the Pirate
ISBN 978 0 7496 6690 3

George and the Dragon
ISBN 978 0 7496 6691 0

Jack the Giant-Killer
ISBN 978 0 7496 6693 4

TALES OF KING ARTHUR

1. The Sword in the Stone
ISBN 978 0 7496 6694 1

2. Arthur the King
ISBN 978 0 7496 6695 8

3. The Round Table
ISBN 978 0 7496 6697 2

4. Sir Lancelot and
the Ice Castle
ISBN 978 0 7496 6698 9

TALES OF ROBIN HOOD

Robin and the Knight
ISBN 978 0 7496 6699 6

Robin and the Monk
ISBN 978 0 7496 6700 9

Robin and the Silver Arrow
ISBN 978 0 7496 6703 0

Robin and the Friar
ISBN 978 0 7496 6702 3

FAIRY TALES

The Emperor's New Clothes
ISBN 978 0 7496 7421 2

Cinderella
ISBN 978 0 7496 7417 5

Snow White
ISBN 978 0 7496 7418 2

Jack and the Beanstalk
ISBN 978 0 7496 7422 9

The Three Billy Goats Gruff
ISBN 978 0 7496 7420 5

The Pied Piper of Hamelin
ISBN 978 0 7496 7419 9

Goldilocks and the
Three Bears
ISBN 978 0 7496 7903 3

Hansel and Gretel
ISBN 978 0 7496 7904 0

The Three Little Pigs
ISBN 978 0 7496 7905 7

Rapunzel
ISBN 978 0 7496 7906 4

Little Red Riding Hood
ISBN 978 0 7496 7907 1

Rumpelstiltskin
ISBN 978 0 7496 7908 8

HISTORIES

Toby and the Great Fire of
London
ISBN 978 0 7496 7410 6

Pocahontas the Peacemaker
ISBN 978 0 7496 7411 3

Grandma's Seaside Bloomers
ISBN 978 0 7496 7412 0

Hoorah for Mary Seacole
ISBN 978 0 7496 7413 7

Remember the 5th
of November
ISBN 978 0 7496 7414 4

Tutankhamun and the Golden
Chariot
ISBN 978 0 7496 7415 1

MYTHS

Icarus, the Boy Who Flew
ISBN 978 0 7496 7992 7 *
ISBN 978 0 7496 8000 8

Perseus and the
Snake Monster
ISBN 978 0 7496 7993 4 *
ISBN 978 0 7496 8001 5

Odysseus and the
Wooden Horse
ISBN 978 0 7496 7994 1 *
ISBN 978 0 7496 8002 2

Persephone and the
Pomegranate Seeds
ISBN 978 0 7496 7995 8 *
ISBN 978 0 7496 8003 9

Romulus and Remus
ISBN 978 0 7496 7996 5 *
ISBN 978 0 7496 8004 6

Thor's Hammer
ISBN 978 0 7496 7997 2*
ISBN 978 0 7496 8005 3

No Dinner for Anansi
ISBN 978 0 7496 7998 9 *
ISBN 978 0 7496 8006 0

Gelert the Brave
ISBN 978 0 7496 7999 6*
ISBN 978 0 7496 8007 7

* hardback